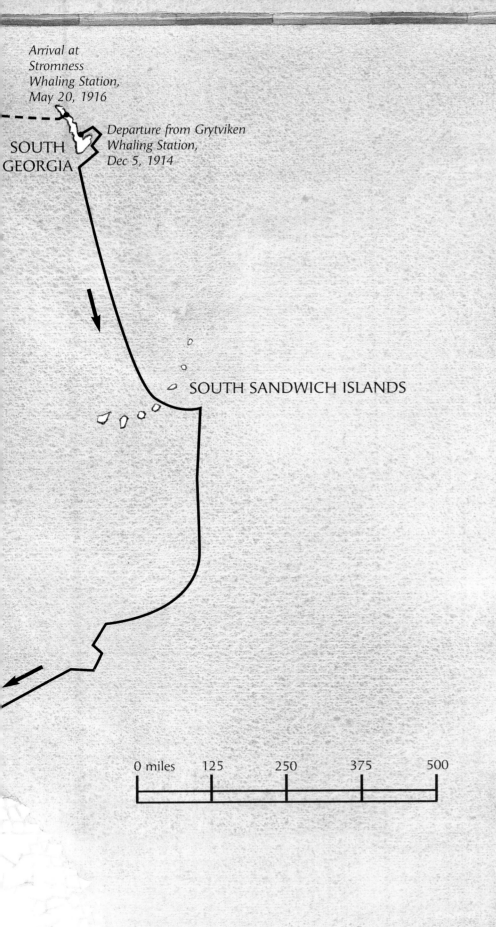

Arrival at Stromness Whaling Station, May 20, 1916

SOUTH GEORGIA

Departure from Grytviken Whaling Station, Dec 5, 1914

SOUTH SANDWICH ISLANDS

| 0 miles | 125 | 250 | 375 | 500 |

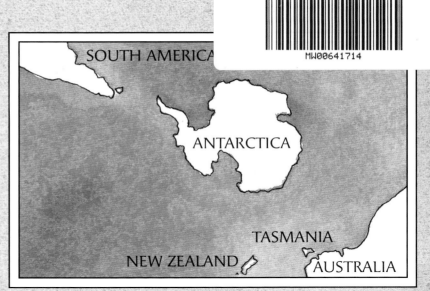

SOUTH AMERICA

ANTARCTICA

TASMANIA

NEW ZEALAND

AUSTRALIA

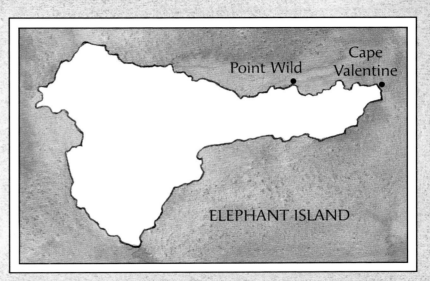

Point Wild

Cape Valentine

ELEPHANT ISLAND

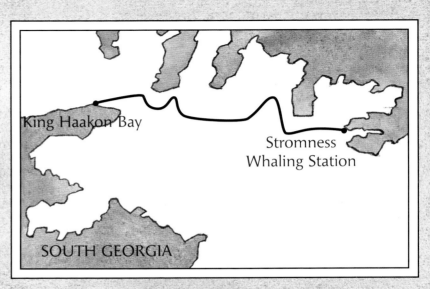

King Haakon Bay

Stromness Whaling Station

SOUTH GEORGIA

To the ship's company of HMS Endurance—M. H.
To Gammack, Jupp, Jones, Nighy and Knox. For tennis and Thursday nights—M. P. R.

ACKNOWLEDGMENTS

The author would like to thank the Commanding Officer of HMS *Endurance* for giving her the opportunity to land on Elephant Island; the Captain of R/V *Laurence M. Gould* for enabling her to track the island's coast by sea; and the United States National Science Foundation for taking her to Antarctica on their Artists & Writers Program.

Frances Lincoln would like to thank Captain Tim Barton RN, William Mills of the Scott Polar Research Institute, and Dr. Jan Piggott of Dulwich College for their help.

First published in the United States of America
in 2001 by Abbeville Press,
22 Cortlandt Street, New York, NY 10007.

First published in Great Britain in 2000 by
Frances Lincoln Limited

Text copyright © Meredith Hooper 2000
Illustrations copyright © M.P. Robertson 2000
Photographs on p 28–29 by Frank Hurley, with the
kind permission of the Royal Geographical Society, London

Printed in Hong Kong

First Edition

ISBN 0-7892-0704-4

1   3   5   7   9   10   8   6   4   2

Library of Congress Card Number: 00-107671

Library of Congress Cataloging-in-Publication Data available upon request

THE ENDURANCE

SHACKLETON'S PERILOUS EXPEDITION IN ANTARCTICA

To Ben -
on your first
Communion, a
real adventure story.
love,
the O'Neils.

MEREDITH HOOPER · M. P. ROBERTSON

ABBEVILLE KIDS · A DIVISION OF ABBEVILLE PUBLISHING GROUP
NEW YORK · LONDON · PARIS

"Stowaway! Stowaway!" The locker lid crashed back and Percy Blackborrow staggered out into the bitter air. For three days he'd been crouching inside the dark locker under piles of clothes while the ship pitched through the ocean. Now he felt so seasick and hungry he didn't mind being discovered.

Suddenly Sir Ernest Shackleton was standing above him, roaring with anger.

"Do you know," bellowed Shackleton, "that on these expeditions we often get very hungry, and if there is a stowaway available he is the first to be eaten?"

Percy looked up. Shackleton was a heavy, powerfully-built man. "They'd get a lot more meat off you, sir!" he said.

Shackleton turned away to hide a grin. "Off to the cook for some food," he said. "Then we'll sign you on."

So nineteen-year-old Percy Blackborrow became the youngest member of Sir Ernest Shackleton's great Imperial Trans-Antarctic Expedition. Shackleton wanted to be the first to walk across the Antarctic continent, 1,800 miles from coast to coast. No one even knew the actual shape of this awesome, ice-covered land at the bottom of the world.

But first Shackleton had to get his wooden ship *Endurance* through the thickest, most dangerous pack ice in Antarctica.

Endurance entered the pack ice in high summer. The floes glittered like endless, ice-white fields. Week after week the ship worked southward, weaving and charging through the sheets of floating ice, finding open patches of indigo blue sea, and dodging icebergs.

Shackleton wanted to get his men ashore as far south as possible, with all their gear and their excited sled dogs. One more day's good sailing should do it, he thought. But pieces of ice crowded around the ship, so they stopped and waited. Pack ice is always on the move, shoving together, then loosening up, as the pieces drift and shift.

But now a gale began blowing, packing the ice tighter.

Before anyone realized what was happening, the ice had hardened around *Endurance* like cement. She was stuck fast, glued into a vast, thick floe. "Frozen in," said the captain, Frank Worsley, "like a nut in a chocolate bar."

The ice drifted, carrying *Endurance* with it. The men could see land in the distance, but they were powerless to go where they wanted. *Endurance* began to drift away from the coast they had striven so hard to reach, back towards the north. The temperature plummeted. Summer was nearly over. A new journey had begun. Unplanned. Unwanted.

Winter came with fearful cold and dreadful darkness. The sun did not rise for seventy-nine days. The dogs curled up out on the floe in "dogloos" made of ice blocks. Inside the warm ship the men discussed what might be happening in the rest of the world, and when they would break free from their lonely prison. They played cards and practical jokes, but they were often bored.

Outside, the silence was eerie. But every now and then ominous moans and clatters in the distance told of huge ice floes grinding together massive blocks of rock-hard ice heaving up in jumbled piles.

One night when the wind howled in the rigging, Shackleton talked to Frank Worsley. "The ship can't live in this," he said. "It's only a matter of time." He paced restlessly in his tiny cabin. "What the ice gets, the ice keeps."

Worsley shuddered at the thought. But they said nothing to the others. Cheerfulness, optimism—that's what mattered. The ice would release its grip. *Endurance* would escape.

Late in the winter the floe trapping *Endurance* broke during a storm. All around, the ice heaped up in confused ridges like giant wrinkled skin. The pieces ground together again, squeezing the ship. *Endurance* was heaved high and thrown on one side, but then she righted herself. But bit by bit her strong, thick beams buckled, bent, then splintered and finally cracked under the terrible, roaring pressure. Day after day the ship groaned like a living thing. The dogs howled. The men watched, helpless.

The end came suddenly one afternoon. Giant fingers of ice forced themselves through the ship's sides. Freezing black water poured into the hold and cabins. Like some terrible animal, the ice fingers held the ship, stopping her sinking.

The men tumbled out onto the floe. Their home had gone. Watching their ship die was horrifying.

Shackleton looked around at his men's tired, anxious faces. Now their safety was all that mattered. They must believe that they would survive.

"Ship and stores have gone," said Shackleton. "So now we'll go home."

The nearest land was hundreds of miles across the pack ice. No one lived there, or ever had. But Shackleton ordered everyone to start marching, dragging the heavy lifeboats across the treacherous icy surface.

The first day they managed less than a mile. The second and third days they traveled only three-quarters of a mile. It was no use. They would have to set up camp.

A thick flat floe was chosen for a campsite. Men walked back to the twisted, broken ship and salvaged what they could.

Life on the floe wasn't too bad. The cook served breakfast at eight o'clock and they sat in their tents as they ate fried seal, tinned fish, or porridge, with lumps of baked dough and tea. For supper they had penguin stew and cocoa. There were plenty of seals and penguins to eat, now that spring was here.

Late one afternoon *Endurance* suddenly upended and sank beneath the ice. They felt very lonely now. The floe they were camping on seemed solid, but it was really just a giant floating raft, drifting ever northward. Underneath their feet lay over two miles of deep, dark ocean.

Shackleton paced the floe as it drifted, zigzaging northward. Summer was almost over. The last of the dogs were shot—there wasn't enough food for them. The men sat in their ragged, dirty clothes, fidgety and anxious as they watched Shackleton. Their lives depended on his decisions.

At the northern edge of the pack ice, an ocean swell bashed at the ice floes, breaking them up. Their floe was drifting ever closer to this treacherous border between ice and open ocean. They would have to take to the lifeboats.

Their floe heaved and tilted in the ocean swell. Bits broke off. Shackleton ordered everyone to sleep fully clothed—with boots on—ready to be out of the tents in thirty seconds. Only absolute necessities could be taken in the boats. But each man still hoarded his own carefully hidden treasures—a photograph, or a Bible, or a tube of toothpaste.

The floe split through the camp. It split again. All around them the ice crashed and lurched. Shackleton watched, waiting for a lead—a gap of clear water. Suddenly it came. The boats were launched; the men scrambled in and bent to the oars.

They had been trapped in the ice prison for 15 months. But the ocean was a much more dangerous, frightening enemy. Their small boats could be easily crushed between jolting, grinding floes. Out in the ocean, the open and overloaded boats could easily be swamped.

By the sixth day of their voyage they were desperately hungry and exhausted. They could hardly speak for thirst, their skin erupted with seawater boils, and they were weak with diarrhea. Spray from heavy seas froze as it fell on their bitterly cold, frostbitten, soaking bodies. Shackleton feared that some of his men would not survive.

Ahead they could see the high mountains and white glaciers of Elephant Island rising bleak and majestic out of the wild ocean. Late in the afternoon a gale began blowing. The sea rose, dangerous and lumpy. They feared being swept in the snowstorms and shrieking wind, past the island, and beyond all hope.

But at dawn the land lay straight ahead. A narrow beach was visible, backed by black cliffs. Riding the surf, they managed to bring all three boats ashore between jagged rocks.

It was land—solid, real, dry land at last. Men staggered along the gray sand, half mad with relief, and laughing, crying. Then they slept, and the sharp stones sticking into their shoulders just made them happier because stones signified the land, not the terrible sea, or the heaving ice.

But the beach was a death trap. High tides could sweep to the base of the cliffs, and the cliffs were too steep to climb. Shackleton forced the men back into the boats.

No one wanted to face the ocean again, but along the coast some of them found a safer place to camp. It was only a low spit of sand and boulders, extending into the ocean, with a glacier at one end and a mess from nesting penguins. They pitched their worn-out tents. In the night a roaring gale ripped a tent and piles of snow covered the sleeping bags. The men were too weary to care.

Elephant Island was uninhabited. Harsh mountains loomed through the swirling clouds. Thick glaciers ground slowly toward the

coast. Some of the men despaired. To go through so much, for this. No one would ever find them here.

The gale blew precious cooking pots into the sea and tossed hard lumps of ice onto their tattered gear. Shackleton gathered everyone, and—shouting against the roar of the wind— told them his final plan: He would fetch help. They would be rescued. With five chosen men he would take the strongest boat and sail to the island of South Georgia, where there were whaling stations, men, and ships.

South Georgia lay 800 miles away across the world's stormiest, wildest ocean. Winter was beginning. The *James Caird* was an open wooden lifeboat, only twenty-three feet long. The risk was terrible, unbelievable.

Shackleton shook hands with each of his men. Standing forlornly on the beach in their thin, patched clothes, they cheered bravely. If anyone could get through, it would be the Boss.

The next morning the pack ice closed in.

Day after day the *James Caird* tumbled and jerked in gale-swept seas. The men could only crawl in the gloomy, soaked little living space below the scrap of canvas deck. Their sleeping bags and clothes were drenched. Once, an enormous wave came from nowhere and swamped the boat. They bailed the freezing water for their lives, and slowly the shuddering, sopping, lurching little craft lifted and became buoyant again. But then their fresh water ran out and they suffered agonies of thirst.

They feared that they would miss the island within the vast ocean and sail on to their deaths. Almost miraculously, on the fifteenth day, they saw black cliffs looming ahead and they shouted for joy. Then a terrible hurricane began roaring in, battering the *James Caird*, almost wrecking them on the very coast they had sailed so far to reach. Desperately bailing water out of their boat, inching back from treacherous rocks in a seething, tormented sea, they pretended that they'd get through. But they all knew they were looking Death square in the eye.

Tired beyond belief, they managed on the seventeenth day to land in a small cove. They were on the wrong side of the island. No one lived there. But they were safe.

The last journey was over land. They had to walk across the glaciers, snow fields, and high mountain passes of South Georgia. A journey that had never been made before.

Shackleton, Frank Worsley and big Tom Crean set off in the moonlight, leaving their three exhausted companions camping under the overturned *James Caird*. They carried a length of rope, the carpenter's axe, a cooker and matches, a watch, and a compass. And in three socks, enough food for six meals.

As darkness fell at the end of the first day, they found themselves high on a mountain pass, on the edge of a razor-sharp ridge of ice. Fog crept up towards them, drifting around their legs. Gingerly, Shackleton climbed over the ridge and began cutting footholds in the ice down the other side. But they weren't descending fast enough. With night coming on, they would freeze at this altitude.

Below, somewhere in the darkness, the ice slope either eased off or steepened into a preci-

pice. They took the risk. Coiling the rope under their bottoms they made themselves into a human toboggan and pushed off, terrifyingly, hair-raisingly fast. At first silent with fear, then yelling with excitement, they hurtled down the slope and fell into a bank of snow. They had descended 1,500 feet in three minutes. Their trousers were in tatters. But they had survived.

At last, thirty-six hours after setting off, they found themselves walking towards the whaling station. Two children saw them.

"Where is the manager's house?" asked Shackleton. The children stared one horrified stare at the three filthy men with matted hair and beards—and fled.

Shackleton, Worsley and Crean had been wearing the same torn, greasy clothes for six months. Their bloodshot eyes blinked wearily in scarred, blackened faces. But they had done what they set out to do.

On Elephant Island the twenty-two men who were left behind built a hut under the remaining boats with walls made of boulders and tent canvas. There was no room to stand upright. It was their bedroom, bathroom, living room, and hospital, all in one dark, filthy, smelly, smoky, greasy space. Some of the men were sick, some injured. The frostbitten toes on Percy Blackborrow's left foot had to be amputated.

The men huddled around the fire, taking turns so everyone had a chance to sit near the heat. The evening meal was over by five o'clock. Then in the gloom they climbed into their wet sleeping bags and sang all the songs they knew, to the twanging sound of a banjo. Every night someone read a recipe out of a little cookbook, and they imagined wonderful meals. Then they lay listening to the beat of the surf, the ice cracking on the glacier, the winter storms hurling stones through the air. The months went by.

Food began to run out. But whenever the sea was clear of ice their leader Frank Wild said, "Roll up your sleeping bags, boys. The Boss may come today."

Week after week, Shackleton tried to find a way to rescue his men still on Elephant Island. The whalers on South Georgia lent a ship, but it couldn't break through the pack ice. Shackleton managed to borrow another ship, and then another, but each time the ice won.

In a last desperate attempt, the Chilean Navy lent a little iron steamer, the *Yelcho*. Shackleton promised not to let it touch the ice. "We shall either die, or return with the shipwrecked men," wrote the Chilean commander to his father.

And this time the weather stayed fine and the pack ice moved away. The men on Elephant Island were sitting down to a stew of old seal bones when they heard a yell of "Ship!" from someone outside. The precious soup was kicked over. They tumbled out of the hut and rushed into the rescue boat. Shackleton allowed no delay. He feared that the pack ice would blow back in, at any moment. Just under an hour from arriving at the camp on the sand spit, the *Yelcho* headed out to sea again.

"I have done it," said Shackleton. "At last. Not a life lost."

It is one of the greatest stories ever of rescue and survival.

SHACKLETON'S IMPERIAL

AUGUST 8 Shackleton and his men sail from England on their expedition to Antarctica, just as World War I begins.

DECEMBER 5 *Endurance* leaves the ice-covered island of South Georgia and reaches the edge of the Antarctic pack ice, in the Weddell Sea, three days later.

JANUARY 18 *Endurance* is frozen in the pack ice at the southern edge of the Weddell Sea.

OCTOBER 27 *Endurance* is crushed by the ice, after drifting north for nine months. Shackleton and his men abandon ship and begin living on the pack ice.

1914   **1915**

APRIL 9 The floe they are camping on reaches the edge of the pack ice. The shipwrecked men finally take to their three lifeboats.

APRIL 15 They land at Cape Valentine on Elephant Island, 160 miles north of the Antarctic Peninsula. Two days later they travel along the coast to Point Wild, where they set up camp.

APRIL 24 Shackleton leaves with five men in the 23-foot *James Caird*, to get help at South Georgia, 800 miles to the east.

MAY 10 The *James Caird* sails across the ocean and reaches South Georgia. The exhausted men come ashore at King Haakon Bay.

1916, continued

THE *AURORA*—SHACKLETON'S SECOND SHIP

Shackleton's plans to walk 1,800 miles across Antarctica included a second ship, the *Aurora*, which landed a party of men at Ross Island, on the opposite side of the continent. These men had orders to walk partway to the South Pole, leaving supplies for Shackleton's party trudging across from the Weddell Sea. The men of the *Aurora* struggled in dreadful conditions to leave supplies, not knowing that Shackleton had never even landed on the continent. Three men died. The survivors were not rescued until January 1917.

TRANS-ANTARCTIC EXPEDITION

OCTOBER 30—NOVEMBER 1
A march begins across the pack ice towards the distant land. The twenty-eight men manage less than two miles, then set up Ocean Camp on the drifting ice.

NOVEMBER 21
Endurance sinks.

DECEMBER 23-29
The pack ice drifts slowly north. They try walking to land again, leaving many things behind, but they fail. They set up Patience Camp on a new floe.

MARCH 23
They see land for the first time on the 139th day of drifting since *Endurance* sank, but it is impossible to reach.

1916

MAY 19-20
Shackleton, Worsley, and Crean walk across South Georgia, forty miles in thirty-six hours, to the Norwegian whaling station at Stromness.

MAY 23
The men marooned at Elephant Island wait to be rescued. Shackleton leaves South Georgia on a first attempt, but cannot get through the ice.

AUGUST 25
Shackleton leaves Punta Arenas, Chile, in the *Yelcho,* on his fourth attempt to reach Elephant Island.

AUGUST 30
All the men are rescued from Elephant Island.

SIR ERNEST SHACKLETON

Ernest Shackleton was born in Ireland on February 15, 1874, moving to England when he was 10. In 1901 he went to Antarctica on an expedition commanded by Robert Scott. Scott chose him to join his small party of three which walked some distance towards the South Pole. Shackleton almost reached the South Pole on his own expedition in 1907-9. Then came the Imperial Trans-Antarctic Expedition, 1914–1917. Shackleton died suddenly in South Georgia on January 5, 1922, aged 47, on his way to the Antarctic again.

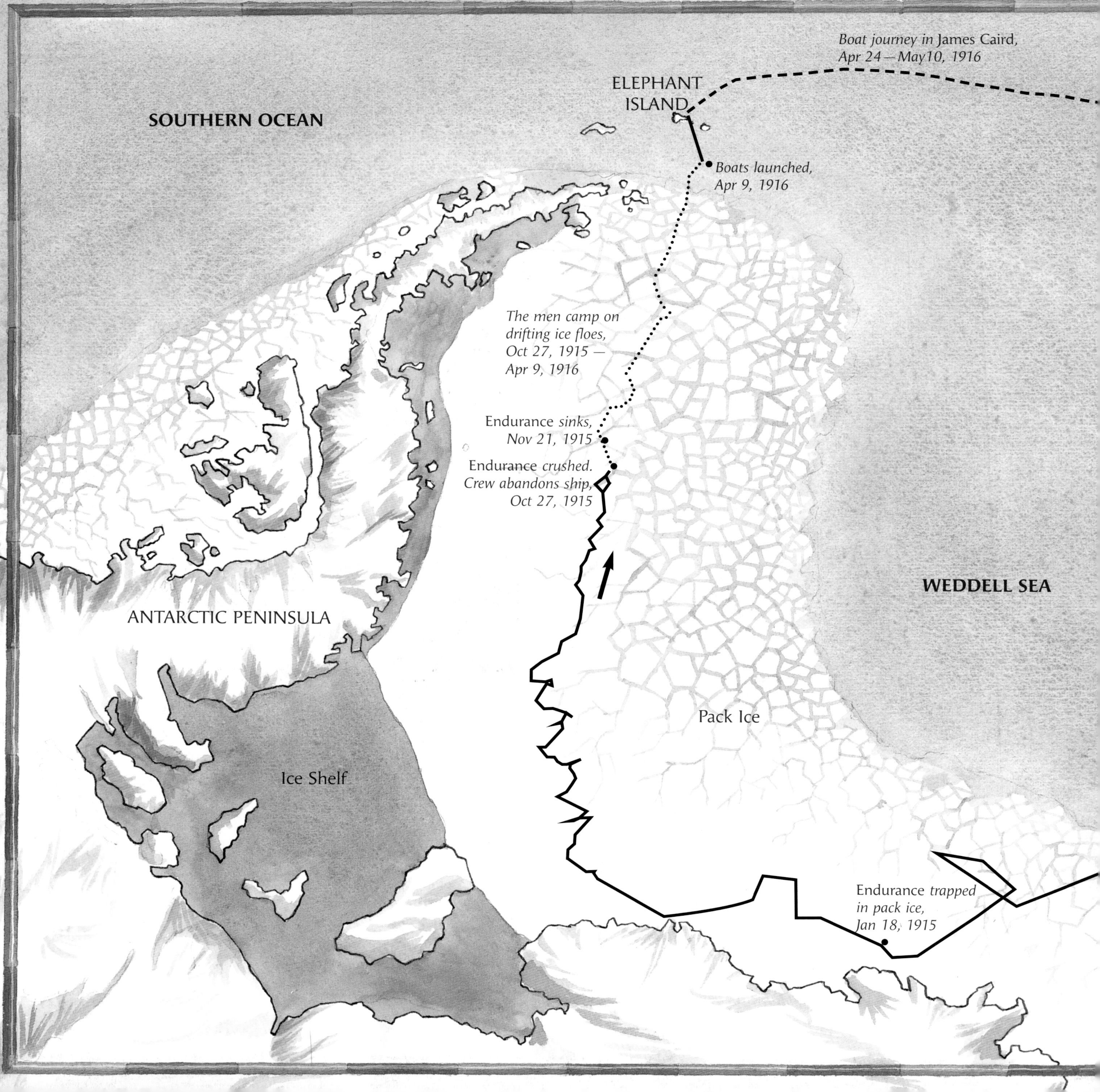

Boat journey in James Caird,
Apr 24 — May10, 1916

**ELEPHANT
ISLAND**

SOUTHERN OCEAN

•Boats launched,
Apr 9, 1916

*The men camp on
drifting ice floes,
Oct 27, 1915 —
Apr 9, 1916*

Endurance *sinks,
Nov 21, 1915*

Endurance *crushed.
Crew abandons ship,
Oct 27, 1915*

WEDDELL SEA

Pack Ice

ANTARCTIC PENINSULA

Ice Shelf

Endurance *trapped
in pack ice,
Jan 18, 1915*